Dan's Darn Dog

The Sound of D

by Joanne Meier and Cecilia Minden · illustrated by Bob Ostrom

The Child's World

Published by The Child's World®
1980 Lookout Drive
Mankato, MN 56003-1705
800-599-READ
www.childsworld.com

The Child's World®: Mary Berendes, Publishing Director
The Design Lab: Design and page production

Library of Congress Cataloging-in-Publication Data
Meier, Joanne D.
  Dan's darn dog : the sound of d / by Joanne Meier
and Cecilia Minden ; illustrated by Bob Ostrom.
    p. cm.
  ISBN 978-1-60253-397-4 (library bound : alk. paper)
  1. English language—Consonants—Juvenile literature.
  2. English language—Phonetics—Juvenile literature 3.
Reading—Phonetic method—Juvenile literature. I. Minden,
Cecilia. II. Ostrom, Bob. III. Title.
  PE1159.M454 2010
  [E]—dc22   2010002910

Printed in the United States of America in Mankato, MN.
July 2010
F11538

NOTE TO PARENTS AND EDUCATORS:

The Child's World® has created this series with the goal of exposing children to engaging stories and illustrations that assist in phonics development. The books in the series will help children learn the relationships between the letters of written language and the individual sounds of spoken language. This contact helps children learn to use these relationships to read and write words.

The books in this series follow a similar format. An introductory page, to be read by an adult, introduces the child to the phonics feature, or sound, that will be highlighted in the book. Read this page to the child, stressing the phonic feature. Help the student learn how to form the sound with her mouth. The story and engaging illustrations follow the introduction. At the end of the story, word lists categorize the feature words into their phonic elements.

Each book in this series has been carefully written to meet specific readability requirements. Close attention has been paid to elements such as word count, sentence length, and vocabulary. Readability formulas measure the ease with which the text can be read and understood. Each book in this series has been analyzed using the Spache readability formula.

Reading research suggests that systematic phonics instruction can greatly improve students' word recognition, spelling, and comprehension skills. This series assists in the teaching of phonics by providing students with important opportunities to apply their knowledge of phonics as they read words, sentences, and text.

This is the letter d.

In this book, you will read words
that have the **d** sound as in:
dog, dig, done, and *dinner*.

Dan and his dad are in the yard. They don't know what to do!

"That darn dog!" says Dad.

"All he does is dig and dig."

"Your mother will be sad when she sees what Dusty has done. Look at her flowers!"

Dan looks at the flowers.

He looks at Dusty.

Dan says, "Come here, Dusty.

Do not dig in the yard.

Let's find a different game."

Dan and Dusty dash around the yard. They run and run.

"This is fun, Dusty! This is what you should do in the yard."

"Dinnertime, Dan," Mother calls from the door. "Please feed the dog and come have dinner. It's getting dark!"

Dad tells Mother, "Dan and Dusty played a new game. Dusty will not dig anymore."

"Hooray!" says Mother. "What a great day."

Fun Facts

What if your dad was president of the United States? Would you want to follow in his footsteps? Two U.S. presidents had sons who decided they wanted to be just like their dads. John Adams was the second president of the United States. John Quincy Adams was his son and became the sixth U.S. president. George H. W. Bush was the forty-first president and the dad of George W. Bush, who became the forty-third.

Did you know that wolves are the ancestors of dogs? Some dogs can live to be 15 years old, but one in Australia survived more than 29 years! One out of every three American families owns a dog. Dogs have a sense of smell that is nearly 1,000 times better than a person's. They can often hear sounds that human beings aren't able to.

Activity

Spending a Day with Your Dad or Granddad
You probably enjoy spending time with your dad or granddad, so set aside a day when just the two of you will do something fun together. Plan a picnic, a project, or a trip to the zoo. Bring a camera so you can take pictures that will remind you of your special day together.

To Learn More

Books
About the Sound of D

Moncure, Jane Belk. *My "d" Sound Box®*. Mankato, MN: The Child's World, 2009.

About Dads

Browne, Anthony. *My Dad*. New York: Farrar Straus Giroux, 2000.

Loomis, Christine, and Jackie Urbanovic (illustrator). *The Ten Best Things About My Dad*. New York: Cartwheel Books, 2004.

Smalls, Irene, and Michael Hays (illustrator). *Kevin and His Dad*. Boston: Little, Brown and Co., 1999.

About Dogs

Beaumont, Karen, and David J. Catrow (illustrator). *Doggone Dogs!* New York: Dial Books for Young Readers, 2008.

Johnson, Bruce, and Sindy McKay. *About Dogs*. San Anselmo, CA: Treasure Bay, Inc. 2009.

Web Sites
Visit our home page for lots of links about the Sound of D:

childsworld.com/links

Note to Parents, Teachers, and Librarians: We routinely check our Web links to make sure they're safe, active sites—so encourage your readers to check them out!

D Feature Words

Proper Names

Dad   Dusty

Dan

Feature Words in Initial Position

dark   do

darn   does

dash   dog

day   don't

different   done

dig   door

dinner

Feature Words with Blends

and   sad

around   should

feed   yard

About the Authors

Joanne Meier, PhD, has worked as an elementary school teacher, university professor, and researcher. She earned her BA in early childhood education from the University of South Carolina, and her MEd and PhD in education from the University of Virginia. She currently works as a literacy consultant for schools and private organizations. Joanne lives in Virginia with her husband Eric, daughters Kella and Erin, two cats, and a gerbil.

Cecilia Minden, PhD, is the former director of the Language and Literacy Program at the Harvard Graduate School of Education. She is now a reading consultant for school and library publications. She earned her PhD in reading education from the University of Virginia. Cecilia and her husband, Dave Cupp, live outside Chapel Hill, North Carolina. They enjoy sharing their love of reading with their grandchildren, Chelsea and Qadir.

About the Illustrator

Bob Ostrom has been illustrating children's books for nearly twenty years. A graduate of the New England School of Art & Design at Suffolk University, Bob has worked for such companies as Disney, Nickelodeon, and Cartoon Network. He lives in North Carolina with his wife Melissa and three children, Will, Charlie, and Mae.